BORN TO DANCE

BORN TO DANCE

Adapted by Aaron Rosenberg

Based on the series created by Chris Thompson

Part One is based on the episode, "Fire It Up," written by Rob Lotterstein

Part Two is based on the episode, "Spirit It Up," written by Darin Henry

DISNEY PRESS

NEW YORK • LOS ANGELES

DANCE IT UP

First Edition
1 3 5 7 9 10 8 6 4 2
V475-2873-0-13196

Library of Congress Control Number: 2013934618
ISBN 978-1-4231-8461-4

For more Disney Press fun, visit www.disneybooks.com
Visit DisneyChannel.com

SUSTAINABLE
FORESTRY
INITIATIVE

Certified Chain of Custody
Promoting Sustainable Forestry

www.sfiprogram.org
SFI-01054

The SFI label applies to the text stock

PART ONE

CHAPTER 1

"I'M SO EXCITED to be back on *Shake It Up, Chicago* after summer break," Rocky Blue told her best friend, CeCe Jones, as they entered the TV dance show's studio through the employees' side entrance. "It's almost as fun as the first day of school."

"I love the first day of school," CeCe agreed, following Rocky up the side stairs. "New clothes, new boys, new teachers who don't know what my mom's signature looks like." They reached the second floor and stepped in through the artists' entrance. "I'm just glad to be away from my mom," CeCe continued, tossing her long red hair. "She's been totally smothering me with too much attention lately."

"That's horrible!" Rocky told her. "Maybe one day you can go to a therapist about that." She pretended to be really upset. "'It was a terrible childhood,'" she choked out, pretending to be CeCe. "'My mother loved me too much.'"

CeCe rolled her eyes. "That's not funny," she insisted. "Ever since we got back from our trip to Japan, she's been like a wool dress on tights—totally clingy."

Rocky frowned. "Well, maybe she just needs a distraction." She gasped, then smiled. "Oooh, what if we find her a boyfriend?"

CeCe sighed. "Rocky, my mom's already

embarrassing. Can you imagine if she actually had a boyfriend?"

Both girls grimaced. "I would rather not," Rocky admitted after a second. "I just ate my breakfast."

"Why can't she just learn to knit?" CeCe declared as they headed down the hallway toward the main stage. "I mean, that would keep her busy, and I'd get some super-cute new sweaters." She paused, running a hand through her hair as she began to ponder the possibility of new outfits. CeCe loved her clothes! "Oooh, hopefully she could make some blue ones, because you know blue really makes my eyes pop. Although, green isn't bad either, because it's my signature color, of course."

Rocky laughed. "CeCe, could you stop making everything about you?" She loved her best friend like a sister, but there was no denying that CeCe was just a little bit self-centered.

While CeCe sputtered a protest, Rocky stepped

past her and brushed through the backdrop separating her from the main stage—and stopped, staring around her in shock. Where before there had been a bright, colorful stage filled with lights, now there was nothing but ashes and blackened fragments. The whole place smelled of smoke and burned fabric. The *Shake It Up, Chicago* stage had burned down!

"Oh, please," CeCe declared, following Rocky out onto the stage without registering the devastation around them. "I do not make everything about me. I never have and I never—" Then it hit her. "Hey, something about me is different in here!"

Rocky shook her head, her long dark hair flying. Sometimes her friend amazed her! "CeCe, big picture," she snapped. "*Shake It Up, Chicago* has burned down!"

CeCe frowned. "Yeah," she replied, "obviously I can see that now!"

The two of them stood there, gazing out over what had been their home away from home and the start of their dream come true. Only now it looked like their dream had just gone up in smoke!

CHAPTER 2

CECE AND ROCKY WANDERED the burned-out ruins of the main stage in a daze. Around them, several of the show's other dancers were also looking about, as were some of the crew. They were all trying to stay out of the way of the firefighters, though. The firefighters were inspecting things and gathering a few bits for evidence, but there wasn't much else they could do. Whatever fire had destroyed the studio was already long since over.

Gary Wilde, the show's host, was near CeCe and Rocky and listening to someone on his cell phone. After a second he hung up and turned to them. The tanned, handsome host looked more frazzled than usual, though as always he didn't have a hair out of place.

"I just got off the phone with the network," he announced loud enough for everyone to hear, "and because of the fire, the show is on indefinite hiatus!"

Rocky stared at him. "What?"

"Relax," CeCe consoled her, "it's not the end of the world."

"Do you know what 'hiatus' means?" her best friend demanded.

CeCe rolled her eyes. "Oh, come on, Rocky! Of course I don't."

Rocky grabbed her shoulders. "It means *Shake It Up, Chicago* is off the air!"

"We're off the air?" CeCe's eyes grew wide, and her face paled. Being a star meant everything to her! "No. No, no, no, no!" she wailed, and stomped. "This cannot be happening. There's got to be something we can do. I know, we can . . . we can . . ." She looked around desperately, then got a mad gleam in her eyes. "We can shoot the show with our phones!" She turned to the other dancers standing around. "Everyone, take out your phones! Start dancing, people! Lights, camera, action! I mean, lights, phones, action!"

Nobody moved. They were all used to CeCe's outbursts, of course. Though this was a little extreme even for her.

Her best friend finally took control. "CeCe," Rocky explained slowly, "there is no 'action.' There are no lights. And in case you haven't noticed, there is no ceiling!"

Gary stepped in. "CeCe, calm down," he told

8

her firmly. "The show's not gone forever. But for the time being, looks like we're all out of a job!" He walked offstage weeping.

As Gary went off crying, Tinka Hessenheffer strolled up, cell phone pressed to her ear.

"It's horrible, Gunther," she reported, her face contorted in an exaggerated pout. "Don't even come down here. Your tears will smear your guy-liner and man-scara." Hanging up, she turned to Rocky and CeCe—and shocked them by giving them both a big hug! "It's okay, girls," she promised in her thick accent. "They will find a way to rebuild, and your talent will be back on the air before you know it."

The girls stared. Blond, bubbly, brightly dressed and extremely catty, Tinka and her matching brother Gunther had been their rivals ever since both pairs had made it on to *Shake It Up, Chicago* at the same time. This was the first time she had ever been nice to them. Something was up!

"Tinka," CeCe said after a second, "I can't believe you're being sweet, supportive, and, dare I say, human-ish."

Tinka laughed and tightened her embrace. "Oh, dear, wonderfully kooky CeCe, it's nice to know we can count on you for a laugh at a tough time like this. God bless you!"

She released them and crossed the stage, leaving Rocky and CeCe to look at each other, totally confused.

"God bless us? What does that she-devil mean by that?" CeCe asked Rocky.

"I guess the fire also melted that big block of ice she calls a heart," Rocky offered. She was always looking for the good in people. Then she returned her thoughts to their current tragedy. "How did all this even happen?" she wondered, looking around.

"We'll probably never know," her friend replied. They stepped over to the side, where the makeup stations had been, and CeCe pointed at what was left of one. "Oooh, look, it's the charred remains of my curling iron. Right here where I left it plugged in next to my hair spray before we left for Japan." Her eyes widened. "Oh, no."

Rocky's mouth fell open. "CeCe," she whispered, horrified. "You burned down *Shake It Up, Chicago*? What're we going to do?"

Just then a fireman stepped up beside them, a clipboard in hand. He looked like he was in charge.

"Don't worry, girls," he reassured them, his voice calm and confident. "I'm Captain Jeremy Hunter. And I will *hunt* down whoever's responsible for this crime. I'm like a dog with a bone." He paused to consider that for a second. "No, I'm like a dog without a bone that wants a bone. And is very good at finding bones. Because . . . well, I'm a dog." He shook his head—apparently he'd even confused himself with that one! "The point is, I will find them and punish them to the full extent of the law."

A quick image came to CeCe—her in an orange jumpsuit, inside a prison cell.

"It wasn't my fault," CeCe wailed in her nightmarish daydream. She clutched at the bars. "It could've happened to anyone who has naturally limp straight hair that requires heat to create volume and curls!" She slumped down against the cell wall.

Jeremy's voice brought her back to reality. "I've got one question," the fire captain told them seriously, "and I want an honest answer—where can I find a good sandwich place around here? Seriously, I'm starving. My stomach's making these horrible sounds." He rubbed his stomach.

"Uh . . . we don't really know any good places," Rocky told him, grinning foolishly. She was a terrible liar!

Next to her, CeCe nodded. "But you know

who would?" she offered. She had no problem lying, and never had. "Ashley. We'll go get her. She's probably in the back somewhere, cleaning candles with oily rags, like always."

The two of them rushed off, leaving Jeremy to frown and make a note on his clipboard. The girls just hoped it wasn't a note about them!

CHAPTER 3

LATER THAT DAY, Rocky's big brother, Ty, and their friend Deuce Martinez stood by the counter at Crusty's Pizza. They were both staring at Gary, who was sitting alone at a table in the pizza parlor. He was still really upset about the *Shake It Up* studio burning down. There were two empty pizza dishes in front of him.

"Deuce," Gary called, his mouth still full

of crust from the last slice, "give me another pie." Deuce's uncle Frank owned Crusty's, and Deuce worked for him after school when he was able to.

"Gary," Deuce said, stepping up beside the table, "you've had two pies already. I'm cutting you off. It's enough."

Gary glared at him, not willing to take no for an answer. "I'll say when it's enough," he declared angrily. "If the camera won't add ten pounds to me, *I'll* add ten pounds to me."

"If he just wanted to add ten pounds," Ty commented from his stool next to the counter, "he should've stopped three slices ago." Deuce rejoined him. "Man," Ty commented, "I've never seen that guy so depressed. You know what he needs?"

Deuce shrugged. "A bucket to throw up in?"

But Ty was serious. "No. A job. You should hook him up."

"Do you really think Crusty's just hires anyone off the street?" Deuce asked him.

Ty grinned at him. "They hired you." He and Deuce had actually competed for the job when the pizza parlor had first opened, but Ty was glad he didn't work there now. It was a lot nicer to just hang out, enjoy a slice, and not have to do anything!

Deuce sighed. "I see your point." He crossed over to Gary again. "Hey, Gary," he said, "I know you're a little out of sorts, so I was thinking if you wanted to, you could work here in the afternoons." Deuce knew his uncle would be okay with that. He trusted Deuce. They were family, after all.

Gary nodded. "Fine, but I'll need a wardrobe, a dressing room, and a parking space," he insisted proudly.

Deuce bit back a smile. "You can have a hairnet, the broom closet, and there's a bike rack out front." He could be a tough negotiator when he had to!

Gary stuck out his hand. "Deal!"

As they shook hands, Deuce wondered if he hadn't just made a huge mistake.

CHAPTER 4

THAT NIGHT, CECE AND ROCKY stepped into CeCe's apartment, only to find CeCe's mom waiting for them.

"Hey, guys!" CeCe's mom said excitedly, hopping up from the living room couch to hug them both. "So how's the first week of school? What's going on with Becca and Kenny? Are they back together or not? And yes she didn't!" She returned to the couch. "Come on, let's catch up on school gossip."

CeCe sat on the couch as well, but she definitely did not want to catch up on school gossip with her mom. "Um, Mom, why don't you get started?" she said instead. "I'll join you after Rocky leaves . . . for college," she added under her breath.

CeCe's mom pretended to be horrified. "Don't *you* ever leave me!" She proceeded to smother CeCe with kisses like she was a little baby. But finally she got up and wandered back toward the kitchen, leaving the girls alone.

"I'm telling you," Rocky declared as soon as CeCe's mom was gone, "she needs a boyfriend."

For once, CeCe wasn't interested in complaining about her mom. "Rocky," she said instead, "I think we have bigger problems than my mother's love life."

Her best friend nodded seriously, moving over to the couch as well. "I know. I'm freaking out, too. What if *Shake It Up, Chicago* never comes back? Where will we dance?" She was starting to get worked up. "I can't be a 'has been' if I've barely been a 'been'!"

CeCe rolled her eyes. "I'm not talking about *Shake It Up, Chicago!*" She dropped her voice to a whisper. "I'm talking about the fact that I could be"–she got loud again–"arrested"–switched back to a whisper–"any second for causing that"–her voice rose until she was practically shouting– "fire."

Rocky shook her head. "I think you whispered the wrong parts," she warned in a whisper of her own.

"I realize that now!" CeCe replied.

"Okay, relax," Rocky reassured her. "They can't pin it on you if they have no proof."

"Proof about what?" asked CeCe's little brother, Flynn, entering the room.

"Nothing," the girls answered together.

Flynn narrowed his eyes. "You two are up to

something," he guessed out loud. "I can feel it in my gut."

"Flynn, you're being ludicrous," his sister scoffed.

But he nodded. "Okay, you just used a three-syllable word. Now I know you're up to something. And I will not rest until I find out what it is!" he declared. "But first . . . I'm going to take a little nap, because I'm tired." He backed toward his room, making the *I've-got-my-eyes-on-you* gesture from his eyes to theirs the whole way.

"As I was saying," Rocky continued once Flynn had left, "you have nothing to worry about because"—she stood and, stepping over to the armchair, reached into her purse and pulled out a very blackened and burned curling iron—"they have no proof!"

CeCe was shocked. "My curling iron?" She rose to her feet. "You stole key evidence from a crime scene?" She was amazed. Rocky was usually such a do-gooder! CeCe was usually the one who broke all the rules!

"I wouldn't say I *stole* it," Rocky argued. "I'm just secretly borrowing it until the end of the investigation. And then throwing it in the lake."

Her best friend laughed, feeling more relaxed than she had all day. "Well, I guess I'm totally in the clear now, thanks to you!" CeCe held out her arms. "Rocky Blue, I love you."

The two girls hugged, then jumped when someone knocked on the apartment's front door.

"Who is it?" CeCe called out.

"Captain Jeremy Hunter," came the reply.

CeCe and Rocky looked at each other, panicked. "The dog with the bone!" CeCe whispered. What was he doing here?

They both glanced down at the curling iron. "Hide the bone!" Rocky ordered. She tossed it to CeCe, who tossed it right back.

"You hide the bone!" she exclaimed.

CeCe broke off to head for the door. Totally flustered, Rocky shoved the burned curling iron under the armchair's bottom cushion just as CeCe opened the door to let Jeremy in.

"I'm just following up on my investigation," he told her as he stepped inside. "Is there a responsible adult here?" He wasn't wearing his fireman's coat and helmet this time, just a fireman's shirt and matching pants.

CeCe shook her head and shut the door. "No, but my mother is. Mom!"

"Coming!" CeCe's mom called back.

Jeremy pulled out a notebook, sat on the couch, and got right to the point. "CeCe, witnesses tell me that you were the last person to leave the studio before vacation."

Again CeCe saw herself in jail. This time she was dragging a tin cup across the bars of her cell.

"Let me out, let me out!" she cried. "I can't take it anymore! I'm going crazy!"

Meanwhile, in the real world, Rocky was defending her. "Well, your witness is a liar, liar, pants on fire," she told Jeremy. "Maybe they did it. You should be looking for a pair of flaming pants."

Jeremy dutifully wrote that down.

Just then CeCe's mom returned. "CeCe! Becca updated her status to 'single'!" Then she noticed Jeremy and stopped. "Well, hello."

Jeremy stood at once. "Hey there! CeCe, you didn't tell me that you had a sister."

CeCe's mom giggled.

Startled, CeCe looked back and forth between the two of them. Both adults were wearing goofy grins. Was it possible? Seeing a way out, CeCe grabbed her mom and all but dragged her across the room.

"Captain Jeremy Hunter," she declared, "allow

me to introduce my available, charming, available, distractingly beautiful, available mother, Georgia. Did I mention she's available?"

She shoved her mom over next to Jeremy, and the two of them smiled at each other. Behind him, Rocky had to work hard not to laugh. She'd seen kids with heavy crushes before, but this was ridiculous!

And her mom just wouldn't stop giggling!

"Yep," Rocky muttered to CeCe as they hurried from the room, "hard to believe she's available."

CeCe's mom and Jeremy barely even noticed them leave.

CHAPTER 5

A FEW DAYS LATER, CeCe and Rocky went to Crusty's to hang out. Deuce and Ty were at the counter, discussing the newest Crusty employee. "So far, Gary's been a terrible pizza maker and a horrible waiter," Deuce told Ty.

"Don't forget an awful bathroom cleaner-upper," Ty pointed out. "Seriously, he put actual cake in the urinal!"

"Well, this job he should be able to do," Deuce

declared. "I mean, who better to be a host . . . than a host?"

They both glanced over toward the stairs that led up to the front door. Gary stood there, holding a pepper grinder like it was a microphone. "Next, coming to table two," he announced, "is a couple that has been waiting for five minutes." A waitress emerged from the kitchen with a fresh pie and walked past Gary. "But first," he called out as she passed, "the Spotlight Pizza of the Week! Put your hands together for Sausage and Pepperoni!"

Several people clapped, even though they looked a little confused.

Deuce shook his head. "He does realize that the microphone he is holding is actually a pepper grinder, right?"

Ty shrugged. "He's asking people to applaud a sausage and pepperoni pizza," he reminded his friend. "I don't think the dude really cares."

Tinka entered the pizza parlor, decked out in bright, contrasting colors and patterns as usual, and approached Rocky and CeCe. "Don't you two look stunning today," she told them. "What's the haps, lady chums?"

CeCe glared at her. "Tinka, this is three days in a row that you've been nice to us," she said. Tinka was never nice to them!

Rocky nodded. "What are you, establishing an alibi before you finally take us out? Just tell us what you want!"

Tinka sighed. "Okay, fine. I would like you to"– she reached into her bag and pulled out two small clumps of blond hair and ribbon, and handed one to each of them–"accept these handmade friendship bracelets, woven from my own hair. Have a nice day, gal pals!"

Rocky inspected hers as Tinka left. "I think these are kind of adorable," she admitted after a second.

CeCe stared at her. "For real?" The bracelets were as bad as Tinka's fashion sense—which was to say, horrible!

Her best friend laughed. "No, I lied!" she said happily.

"What, you lied?" CeCe studied her. Tinka being nice and Rocky lying? What was going on around here?

"Okay, at first," Rocky explained, scooting her chair closer, "I felt really bad for taking that curling iron. But between you and me, it was kind of exciting. I feel so"—she giggled a little—"dishonest. I haven't felt this kind of rush since I led the team to victory in the Academic Decathlon!" She paused a second, then corrected herself: "Actually, we came in second place. I lied again!" She was positively giddy!

Shaking her head, CeCe noticed her mom and Jeremy sitting at a nearby table, smiling goofily at each other. "Ugh, look at them," she told Rocky. "I don't think I like where this is heading."

"Would you rather be heading to a prison cell?" her best friend asked. Which was a good point.

Flynn walked in and headed straight for CeCe's mom and Jeremy.

"Hey, Little Fire Hydrant!" Jeremy exclaimed.

"Jeremy, you're a good guy," Flynn told him, "but we're not at the nickname stage yet. And if we do get there, it sure as heck won't be something that a poodle pees on."

Jeremy laughed. "Wow, you sound like a thirty-five-year-old man trapped inside a child's body. Don't worry, I'll save you." He grabbed Flynn, lifted him off the ground, and started shaking him. "Hurry up, get me out of this kid!" he said in a fake voice. "I've got to go diversify my portfolio!"

Flynn smiled patiently. Adults could be such

kids at times! "If you're done mocking me, Chief," he said when Jeremy finally set him back down, "I'm about to pour some high-octane knowledge into your mind tank." He held up a pair of large photos. "I found a discrepancy in your file. In this photo, there's something suspicious on the makeup table. But in the later photo—it's mysteriously disappeared."

"Missing evidence," Jeremy said, still chuckling as he took the photos. "You're just too cute! You know, maybe I should just make you my little assistant." He glanced at the pictures, then looked again, now completely serious. "Okay, I see it now. I've got to get down to the studio right away!" He hurried out.

"Did you hear what he just said?" CeCe asked Rocky in a panic. "I can't go to prison! I do not look good in jumpsuits. And I do not look good in orange. And I *really* do not look good in orange jumpsuits!"

"CeCe, relax," Rocky told her. "There's absolutely nothing to worry about." She hesitated for a second, then admitted, "Sorry, lying again. Yeah, you're dead meat."

CHAPTER 6

THAT NIGHT, CECE PACED around the kitchen, waiting impatiently to talk to her mom. But her mom was in the middle of a phone call with Jeremy.

"No, Jeremy, you hang up," her mom said. She giggled. "No, you hang up. No, you hang up." This discussion had been going on for twenty minutes.

Finally, CeCe couldn't take another minute of

the back-and-forth. She grabbed the phone out of her mom's hand. "No, *I'll* hang up." And she did.

"Well, what's the matter with you?" her mom asked.

"Thank you for finally asking," CeCe snapped. "I've been upset and pouting and acting weird all day, and you haven't even noticed." She slumped onto one of the kitchen chairs.

CeCe's mom shook her head. "Oh, I thought you were just being a teenager." She sat down beside CeCe. "Okay, time for a mother-daughter talk."

"I think I might have caused the fire at the *Shake It Up* studio," CeCe blurted out.

Her mother stared at her, then corrected her earlier statement. "Okay, time for a *lawyer-daughter* talk."

"It was an accident," CeCe explained. "I think it might have been my curling iron that started the fire. I need to tell Jeremy." It felt so good to finally admit that!

Her mom apparently didn't agree. "But you don't know for sure that's what caused it," she argued. "So why mention it right now? Let's just let them finish their investigation." She frowned. "'Cause nothing puts a damper on a new relationship like having to lock up your new girlfriend's daughter!"

CeCe couldn't believe what she was hearing. "But, Mom, what if it's all my fault?"

"And what if it's not?" her mom countered. "And besides, it's still an accident. And you shouldn't feel bad; accidents happen." She rubbed CeCe's arm, trying her best to console her.

Flynn wandered in just in time to hear that last part. "Really, CeCe?" he said, shaking his head and sounding like a disappointed parent. "An accident at your age?"

CeCe glared at him. "Not *that* kind of

accident!" Sometimes her little brother could be such a pain!

"So what were you two talking about?" Flynn asked.

CeCe and her Mom looked at each other, trying to quickly think of something to say.

"Lip gloss," CeCe answered at once. Unfortunately, her mom blurted out "Reincarnation" at the same time.

They looked at each other.

"Reincarnation," CeCe said quickly.

"Lip gloss," her mom corrected herself, again at the same time.

They paused a second.

"Reincarnated lip gloss," CeCe finally managed. CeCe's mom nodded, playing along, hoping they sounded believable.

Flynn did not look convinced, though. "I see you've roped Mom into your little house of lies," he commented. "I'm used to this type of behavior from CeCe, but I expected more from you"–he focused on his mom–"Mother!"

Then he turned and huffed off back to his room. CeCe and her mom just watched him go, mystified.

CHAPTER 7

"GO AHEAD, GUNTHER! I'll meet you in the library!" Tinka called over her shoulder as she strolled down the hall at school the next day. "I just want to hand out these whole-grain, fruit juice–sweetened cupcakes to the coolest kids in school!" And she turned toward CeCe and Rocky, a cupcake in each hand.

"Oh, come on!" CeCe declared, slamming

one hand dramatically against a nearby column. "Enough is enough!"

"Yeah," Rocky agreed. "Tinka, you don't compliment people."

"And you definitely don't bake goodies," CeCe added.

Rocky nodded. "And you don't do CeCe's homework for her."

CeCe frowned at her friend. "All right, Rocky," she said quickly, "let's not criticize *everything* she does." Then she turned her attention back to Tinka. "Tinka, we want to know what's going on with you, right now."

Tinka sighed, all the pep vanishing in an instant. "Fine," she declared, "I will tell you. You will notice there is no cupcake for Gunther because . . . Gunther is . . . gone-ter!"

Rocky and CeCe looked at each other. "What are you talking about?" Rocky asked. Which made CeCe feel better. If Rocky didn't understand, there was no way she would have!

"Gunther has gone back home to the old country," Tinka explained, "to take care of Great-Great-Grandma, help on the farm, and, hopefully, quell the revolution."

Now Rocky understood. "So you thought you'd bake us some cupcakes, and we'd just forget about all the mean, nasty, cruel things you've said and done to us over the years, and we'd all be best friends?" Unbelievable!

And yet, she wasn't surprised when Tinka smiled and said, "Exactly!" She handed them each a cupcake, and they accepted the baked goodies automatically. "So what are we thinking? Party of slumber tonight?"

But CeCe wasn't falling for it. "Sorry, Tinka," she replied, "we cannot be manipulated that easily. Our friendship cannot be bought, it needs to be earned."

Tinka frowned. "Fine!" She snatched back

the cupcakes—just as Rocky was about to take a bite of hers!—and stormed off.

For half a second Rocky was upset about the cupcake. She was almost eating that! Then she realized what Tinka had said, and what it could mean for them. Especially for CeCe!

"CeCe, this is the break we need!" she told her best friend, dragging her over to a nearby bench so they could talk in private. "We'll pin the whole fire on Gunther! It's not like they can question him. No one even knows how to pronounce the name of that country, let alone how to find it!"

Surprisingly, for once it was CeCe who was the voice of reason. "Whoa there, Pinocchio," she warned. She took a deep breath. "It's time I take responsibility for what I did and accept whatever punishment I deserve."

"CeCe, I cannot let you do that," Rocky argued. Talk about role reversal! Then Rocky explained her reasoning: "How can you be my dance partner if you're rotting away in a prison cell wearing a hideous orange jumpsuit?"

CeCe considered that. "Well, maybe you can go to prison with me," she offered, "and we can do those disturbingly accurate Michael Jackson dance re-creations with all the other inmates. It could be a lot of fun!"

She had a brief flash of her in prison again, but this time Rocky was with her, and other inmates surrounded them. And they were all dancing to "Thriller."

"Okay, you're right," CeCe decided. "We've got to be ready with the Gunther cover story for when they come and get me!"

Rocky patted her hand reassuringly. "Okay, don't be so paranoid. It's not like someone's going to walk in here right now to come and take you to jail."

Just then, Flynn stopped beside the bench.

CeCe stared at her little brother. "Flynn, what are you doing here?" He didn't even go to this school!

Flynn smiled. "Captain Jeremy sent me to come and get you!" he told them happily.

CeCe shot Rocky a look, as if to say, *Oh, yeah? Who's being paranoid now?*

CHAPTER 8

DEUCE EMERGED FROM the kitchen at Crusty's to find Gary standing at the bottom of the stairs, as usual. But this time there was a long line of people behind him.

"Gary," Deuce asked, "why aren't you seating anyone who's waiting for a table?" Then he glanced around—and saw exactly why. "Where are the tables?" he demanded.

"You'll see," Gary promised. He had a huge

grin on his face. He held out a hand. "Now, if you'll just hand me my pepper grinder, I have some hosting to do." Deuce found himself slowly handing over the pepper grinder, even though he wasn't sure why. "Welcome back, everybody!" Gary announced. "And now, put your hands together for the Elektrolytes!"

The dance troupe leaped down the stairs and onto the cleared center of the restaurant floor. They were all wearing matching outfits with green pants, T-shirts patterned to look like a white button-down shirt and a black tie, white gloves, sneakers, and black letterman jackets.

They went into their routine, moving together in rhythm—and then the lights went out! But it was all part of the show—their white gloves now glowed green or blue, and the dancers proceeded to perform by making the glowing images dance over and around each other to the music's beat. It was a great show, Deuce had to admit.

Still, he was annoyed. The dancers finished, the lights came back on, everyone applauded, and the Elektrolytes trotted back up the stairs and out. It was almost as if the performance had never happened! Then Deuce turned to Gary.

"Gary," he said angrily, "you didn't ask my permission to have a dance performance."

"I know," Gary admitted, "but they were already booked for *Shake It Up, Chicago*, and I didn't want to disappoint them."

Deuce shook his head. That was the last straw! He took the pepper grinder from Gary, handing it behind him to Ty—who immediately put some pepper on his salad. But Deuce was focused on his troublesome new employee.

"Here's the deal," he told Gary. "This isn't working out."

Gary frowned. "What do you mean?" He looked genuinely confused.

Deuce tried again. "You're not needed any-more."

But Gary shook his head. "Not following."

Deuce sighed. "Crusty's is downsizing," he explained.

"Still not getting your point," Gary replied. Man, this guy was dense!

Finally, Deuce frowned. Time to use language a TV host would understand! "Gary, you've been cancelled."

Gary's confusion cleared, and he scowled. "Well!" he snapped. "Then if you'll excuse me, I'm going to go clean out my dressing room!" He stormed off.

"It's a broom closet!" Deuce shouted after him.

CHAPTER 9

CECE AND ROCKY stood uncomfortably with Gary and Tinka on the edge of the burned-down *Shake It Up, Chicago* main stage. CeCe's mom and Jeremy were talking quietly nearby.

"People!" Flynn called out to the crowd. He was between the two little groups, a notepad and pen in hand. "May I have your full attention, please?"

Everyone turned to watch as Flynn paced

across the floor. "I'd like to thank you all for coming," he told them. "I have to admit, this is one of the toughest fire investigations I've ever done." Of course, it was also the *only* fire investigation he'd ever done, but he wasn't going to mention that! "There were times when I thought I would never figure out exactly what happened." He paused for a second, then admitted, "And I was right. I didn't." Then he smiled. "But my buddy Jeremy here did."

Jeremy smiled at Flynn. "That's right, Fire Alarm Flynn!"

Flynn gave him a sad little smile. "Jeremy! Buddy! This whole nickname thing? It's just not happening and it never will." Jeremy nodded in agreement. Flynn then held up his notebook and announced, "I will now reveal that the cause of the fire was—"

CeCe couldn't take it anymore. "Me!" she interrupted. "It was me! It's all my fault. I left my curling iron plugged in, and the next thing you know, *Shake It Up, Chicago* is toast! Burned toast!" She felt terrible, but at least she didn't have to keep lying!

Behind Jeremy, CeCe's mom gasped. "CeCe, how could you?" she asked, doing her best to look surprised at her daughter's confession. "And why didn't you tell me about this sooner?" She turned to Jeremy. "I would've come to you the minute I heard," she claimed.

Rocky couldn't let her best friend take all the blame. "Okay," she declared, edging forward, "she's not the only one at fault! I lied! I stole the evidence and hindered the investigation. I'm a lying, stealing hinderer." She could barely believe the words that were coming out of her mouth. How had she sunk so low?

Then, surprisingly, Tinka stepped between them. "No, I simply can't let you two do this," she told CeCe and Rocky. "They're covering for me," she continued, now speaking to Jeremy. "I'm the one who left my curling iron plugged in, even though"—and she glared at CeCe—"only a complete imbecile would do that. It's all my fault!" She held out her arms, crossed at the wrists. "Take me away!"

All three girls began arguing about why they were the one at fault, until Jeremy stopped them. "Girls," he asked, "what are you talking about? The fire wasn't started by a curling iron. It was started by a faulty tanning bed!"

CeCe and Rocky both felt a sense of relief.

Gary, on the other hand, looked suddenly concerned. But just as tan as ever.

"A faulty tanning bed?" he asked. "Wow, when I find out what narcissistic idiot was using a tanning bed at the studio, they are going to be in . . . a reasonable and forgivable amount of trouble!" He turned and quickly walked off.

Jeremy shook his head. "Okay," he said to everyone who was left, "well, now that the case is closed, I was thinking I could take everyone out for a fancy dinner to celebrate."

Flynn smiled. "Sounds good to me, Inspector Smoke Detector!"

Jeremy frowned. "You know, you're right," he told Flynn as he took CeCe's mom's arm to lead her out. "This whole nickname thing? Let's let it go."

The three of them headed toward the exit, happy that the investigation was over. Then Rocky turned to Tinka. So did CeCe.

"I can't believe you were willing to take the blame for this," Rocky told Tinka. "Why would you do that?"

Tinka gave a little laugh. "Well," she answered, "now that Gunther is gone, and there's no *Shake It Up, Chicago*, I have nothing to do anyway. Prison would be a welcome relief." She laughed again, and drew herself up proudly. "At least for a while. Wouldn't be the first time I tunneled my way to freedom!"

But CeCe shook her head. "Yeah, I'm not buying it. I think you did it because you know our friendship cannot be bought, it needs to be earned." She was on one side of Tinka, with Rocky on the other, as she continued, a big smile breaking out across her face, "And, Tinka—you earned it!"

She and Rocky converged on their former nemesis in a group hug.

For a second, Tinka melted. Then she stiffened. "Okay, yeah," she declared, "this whole friendship thing is not going to work." But the two girls kept hugging her. "Seriously," she demanded, "get off of me!" CeCe and Rocky didn't stop, and Tinka softened again. "Okay, maybe just two more seconds," she allowed. "But then I really must put an end to this." Still, she had to admit, at least to herself, it actually was pretty nice having girlfriends!

♪ ♪ ♪

"I feel terrible about firing Gary," Deuce told Ty the next day at school as they walked down the hall.

"Ah, don't sweat it," Ty responded. "I got him a new gig. Listen to this!"

Just then, Gary's voice came over the school loudspeaker!

"I'm your host, Gary Wilde," he stated, "with today's announcements! Coming up for lunch, flank steak and corn. Can I get an 'Oh yum!'?" Several people cheered and clapped, including both Ty and Deuce. But then Gary continued, "And now, a Public Service Announcement: Avoid eating at Crusty's, because Deuce Martinez practices his kissing skills on the pizza dough!" Everyone laughed. Except Deuce.

"Well," he said instead, "at least he's not holding a grudge."

Ty grinned. "He's also not writing his own material," he told his best friend. "I gave him that kissing line." He made a kissy face at Deuce before laughing and running off.

PART TWO

The *Shake It Up, Chicago* studio burned down!

Not only were Rocky and CeCe out of a job,
but Tinka was also being . . . nice!

CeCe feared that she might have accidentally
caused the fire!

If CeCe burned down the studio, she could go to jail . . .
and orange jumpsuits were *so* not her style!

Flynn shared hot new evidence with the firefighter.

The evidence revealed a clue as to how the fire started!

Tinka tried to buy Rocky's and CeCe's friendship
with cupcakes. How ... sweet?

The fireman discovered the cause of the fire. Would
CeCe's and Rocky's dreams go up in smoke?

Rocky and CeCe joined the school spirit squad—
minus the spirit!

Rocky gave the spirit squad a pep talk before the pep rally.

Rocky wanted to steal the shining moment for herself!

Deuce and Dina were two peas in a . . . pep rally!

The squad didn't miss a beat in their peppy performance!

It was finally time for the showstopping moment . . .

Rocky and CeCe rooted for Margie as her spirit soared!

Margie slid into a split! She felt triumphant . . . even
though she couldn't get up.

CHAPTER 1

"HEY, CECE," ROCKY CALLED out as she let herself into her best friend's apartment, "I got your text and I'm here to help you cram for your science test!" She dropped her backpack on the couch and danced over toward the kitchen, holding up a poster she'd made—it had a wheel and a spinner on it, and science terms next to each section of the wheel. "Who's ready to play Wheel of Physics?" Rocky sang. She loved school and was thrilled to help CeCe study! Her excitement faded, however, when she reached the kitchen and saw that next to CeCe at the table were their friends Deuce, Dina, and Tinka. "Okay," she asked, the smile dropping from her face, "what's going on?"

"Rocky," CeCe told her seriously, "we're concerned about you. This is an intermission!"

Deuce rolled his eyes. "Intervention," he corrected.

CeCe didn't miss a beat. "That too!" she agreed. Standing, she stepped over to the counter across from Rocky. "Ever since *Shake It Up, Chicago* burned down," she explained, "you have shown all the classic symptoms of"—she paused dramatically—"dance withdrawal."

"Mood swings," Deuce's girlfriend, Dina, added from the table, "cold sweats, dancing at inappropriate times." Like Deuce, Dina had a pair of headphones around her neck.

Tinka nodded. "Like your oddly shaped big toe," she told Rocky, "it's not pretty." It was still strange to think of Tinka as a friend after all the trouble she and her brother Gunther had given Rocky and CeCe over the years. But she was here, apparently to help.

CeCe was more sympathetic. "But, Rocky, you're not alone," she promised her best friend. "I went through the same thing, and you helped me get through my funk, and now we're going to help you through yours."

Rocky shook her head. "Okay, guys, this is ridiculous!" she told them. "I'm in complete control of my dancing. I can stop whenever I want."

Dina winced. "Ooh, classic denial." She turned to her boyfriend and commanded, "Deucie, hit it!"

Deuce had his cell phone in hand, with the music player open. He hit PLAY and music poured forth. Instantly Rocky's shoulders started twitching to the beat. She tried to control it, but next thing they knew she was up on her feet and dancing around, clapping her hands and stomping. She bounced into the kitchen, still on fire, and called to the others, "Okay, don't just stand there, help me!"

At once her friend rushed to restrain her. It wasn't easy, though—Rocky wanted to dance!

There was no more denying it. She clearly was going through dance withdrawal.

CHAPTER 2

THE NEXT DAY AT SCHOOL, the girls were still trying to figure out what to do. "Look, I want to dance just as much as you do, Rocky," CeCe said as they walked down the stairs and into one of the main hallways. "And here's an idea. What about community theater?"

Rocky considered that, then nodded. "Huh. That could work," she admitted. She was surprised. CeCe had actually come up with something useful!

Her friend grinned at her. "Great! We can audition for *Beauty and the Beast*!" She tossed back her long red hair and smiled. "I can play Beauty and you can be the–"

Rocky interrupted her quickly. "Don't even say it," she warned, raising her hands, her fingers out like claws.

CeCe's smile faltered a little, but she tried to save it. "See," she offered weakly, "you're a natural!"

Rocky turned and walked away, toward a bench off to the side.

CeCe followed her, of course. "Come on, I'm trying," she pointed out, sitting beside Rocky. "What, do you think some big dance opportunity is just going to waltz right up to us?"

Just then they heard noise coming down the hall. A second later, six girls in matching outfits– blue John Hughes High School Bulldogs T-shirts, darker blue skirts, red tights, and white tennis shoes—marched around the corner. It was the school's Spirit Squad!

"Go team, fight team, get in the spirit, yay," the girls called out as they walked into the center of the hall. But they said it without any enthusiasm, like they were reciting some boring speech. All in all, they looked like they'd rather be anywhere but there, and doing anything but that.

CeCe and Rocky just stared.

The girl in front, named Margie, stepped forward. "Come see the Spirit Squad perform at the pep rally this Friday," she announced with the same lack of enthusiasm. She halfheartedly raised one fist—"Go"—then let it drop—"or don't."

Rocky sighed dramatically as the Spirit Squad members wandered away. "Oh yes," she told CeCe, "the Spirit Squad. You know, they should have their own TV show: *So You Know You Can't Dance.*"

CeCe, however, had just had a brilliant

idea. "Actually," she replied, "I know two amazing dancers on that squad."

Rocky studied her. Was this a joke? "Who?" she asked finally.

Her friend beamed at her. "Me and you!"

"Huh." Rocky considered that, then shrugged. "It's better than being the Beast."

She stood and made her way down the hall. CeCe was right behind her. Could this be the answer to their dancing woes? she wondered. At least Rocky seemed interested—that was a start!

CHAPTER 3

"AH, DEUCE, DINA," Tinka called out that afternoon as she crossed the floor of Crusty's Pizza Parlor, the gang's favorite after-school hangout. She stopped at the corner booth the couple was sharing and leaned against the edge of Dina's seat. "So, what are you two love partridges up to?"

"Just sharing an after-school smoothie," Deuce told her. Sure enough, there was a smoothie on the table between them, with two straws.

Dina smiled at him. "Half the carbs, twice the love," she announced.

Tinka smirked. "You left out 'best shared with friends,'" she added, starting to slide into the booth as well. But Dina didn't budge—if anything, she leaned back out, and Tinka found herself bouncing off the other girl and landing on her butt on the floor!

"Sorry, Tinka," Dina told her. She didn't sound very sorry, though, as she continued, "This is a booth for two. So go crack open a fresh box of 'beat it.'"

Tinka rose to her feet, straightened her skirt, and walked off with as much dignity as she could manage. Which wasn't much, under the circumstances. Deuce stared after her, then turned to his girlfriend. Dina had gone right back to enjoying their smoothie.

"Isn't this smoothie juicy, Deucie?" she asked happily.

"Well, sweetie," he managed to reply after a second, "it's certainly sweeter than you are. How could you be so mean to Tinka?"

Dina frowned. "Mean? Since when is pushing and insulting someone . . ." She stopped, surprised. "Oh, I see your point." Dina wasn't mean by nature. She was just brash, and very direct. Deuce liked that about her . . . most of the time.

But right now he felt bad for the blonde they'd just dissed. "The poor girl's got three strikes against her," he reminded Dina. "Her brother's gone, her dance show's off the air, and her clothes make her look like a box of melted crayons. Would it be so horrible for us to let her join us?"

Dina smiled at him. She loved that for all his tough-guy image, Deuce was a real sweetheart underneath. "You're right, Deucie," she declared. "Let's cut that sequined sad sack some slack!" She turned to look around. "Tinka," she called, "would you–"

"I'd love to!" Tinka answered. Tinka was already in the booth next to Deuce! And from somewhere, she had produced a straw of her own—a big pink glittery one—which was already in their smoothie!

Dina tried to smile back. But inside she wondered if this was really going to be such a good idea.

♪ ♪ ♪

Meanwhile, CeCe's little brother, Flynn, was returning to their apartment when he spotted a boy emerging from the apartment next door.

"Hey," Flynn called out. "I don't know you."

"I just moved in," the other boy answered. He looked to be about Flynn's age, skinny, with dark hair and glasses.

Flynn smiled. "Cool, a new kid in the building. And lucky you, you're me-adjacent." He stepped forward and offered his hand. "Flynn's the name, and fun's the game."

"Oh, hi," the other boy responded. He didn't shake hands. "My name is—"

"I'll just call you Freckles," Flynn interrupted. Even though the other boy's dark skin didn't show a single freckle. "So, you want to hang out?"

"Freckles" frowned. "Thanks, Flynn," he said finally, "but I don't think so. You kind of have a reputation."

Flynn smirked. "For being really cool?"

But Freckles shook his head. "Actually, I hear you have a little bit of a revolving door in your sandbox."

"What does that mean?" Flynn asked. Whatever it was, it didn't sound good!

Freckles explained. "You make a friend, have a few laughs, get bored, and move on to someone new." He tapped his own narrow chest. "I'm looking for an LTBFF."

Flynn had no idea what that meant. "Lettuce, tomato, bacon, french fries?" he guessed.

"No," Freckles corrected. "Long-Term Best Friends Forever. Nothing personal, but I'm not nine anymore. I need someone who can go the distance."

Flynn studied this new kid. Who was this guy? Still, he was offended to have anyone think he wasn't friend material. "Okay," he started, "I mean, this is ridiculous. I can totally—"

"Not gonna happen, dude," Freckles interrupted. Then he walked away!

"Oh, forget you," Flynn muttered after him. Whatever! He had plenty of long-term friends! Who did this guy think he was?

Entering his apartment, Flynn picked up the phone. "Revolving door in my sandbox," he said as he dialed. "What a crock. Hi, Mr. Chang," he said as soon as the person on the other end picked up. "May I speak to Edwin, please? It's his LTBFF, Flynn." Then the other person started speaking, and Flynn's smile disappeared, replaced by a confused look. "The Changs moved?" he repeated, his eyes going wide. "Three years ago?"

How could Edwin not have told him? Flynn wondered as he hung up.

And was Freckles right about him?

No! And he was going to prove it!

CHAPTER 4

AROUND THE SAME time, CeCe and Rocky walked into the school gym. The Spirit Squad was there, but they weren't exactly practicing. Instead they were sprawled on the bleachers. Some of them were talking, some were applying makeup, some were texting, and one girl was reading. One was even taking a nap!

"Um, hi," CeCe called out as they approached the other girls. "I'm CeCe and this is Rocky.

And we want to join your Spirit Squad."

"Yeah," Rocky added, "I think we can really help you guys. I mean, we know style. We know rhythm—"

"And we know how to keep your tights from getting stuck up your butt," CeCe added. That had been one of the most important things she'd learned from being a dancer on *Shake It Up, Chicago*!

Rocky smiled. She'd saved the best for last! "And we'll teach you everything there is to know about dancing!" she offered.

"That is so awesome of you guys!" one of the girls, a blonde named Crystal, told them. "But we're good." She went right back to texting her friend.

Rocky was surprised by their bad attitude. "Aren't you guys maybe just a little bit worried about embarrassing yourselves at next week's pep rally?" she asked.

"Not at all," Crystal replied. She and Margie shared a smile. "We're calling in sick that day!" All the girls laughed.

All except CeCe and Rocky. "Then why did you even join the Spirit Squad?" CeCe wanted to know.

"Uh, for the free period," Margie answered, as if it were obvious. "Because otherwise, we'd have to take gym, and that is *not* how we roll." The other members all nodded.

"Look," Rocky tried again, "you guys really need some help, and we really need an outlet for our dance . . . but mostly, you guys *really* need some help. So maybe we could just give it a try?"

CeCe didn't see much point in continuing, but she was a loyal friend, so she backed Rocky up. "Yeah, show us the one dance you do that can really make a crowd roar," she said. "And not with laughter," she added.

"There is something we've been working on during practice to pump up the football team," Crystal admitted. She stood, as did the other members, and they started to chant, raising their arms as they did.

"Good enough!" they called out weakly. "Good enough! Good enough!"

"Or not," Margie added, waving it off. The girls draped themselves about the bleachers again and returned to their previous activities.

CeCe had seen enough. "Oh, forget it!" she told Rocky. "You can be Beauty. Let's get out of here!"

She turned to go, but Rocky grabbed her arm. "No," she said quietly. "I think we can really turn this squad around." Leave it to Rocky to want to help. She was such a do-gooder!

"All right, listen up, ladies!" Rocky announced, turning her attention back to the members of the Spirit Squad. "'Good enough' is not good enough. Not in Rocky Blue's book. With just a little effort, you guys could be great. Everyone deserves at least one shining moment, and I think this pep rally could be yours. All right, now, who's ready to shine?"

The girls just looked at her.

CeCe could tell Rocky's inspirational speech wasn't going to work. She had a different idea of how to motivate the other girls. "If you say yes," she offered, "Rocky will do all your home-work for a week!"

That, at least, got the squad cheering.

It looked like Rocky and CeCe were on the squad!

CHAPTER 5

"**YOU SURE ABOUT** the neon turquoise?" Dina asked. It was a few days later, and she and Tinka were sitting on a couch near her locker toward the end of the school day. They'd been looking at a clothing catalog. "I was thinking basic black," Dina continued. She had to admit, hanging out with Tinka was a lot of fun!

Tinka wrinkled her nose like she'd smelled something terrible. "Black boots with black jeans?"

She sneered, then laughed. "Seriously, Dina, your taste in clothes is almost as bad as your taste in—" She broke off as she spotted Dina's boyfriend approaching them. "Oh, hi, Deuce!"

"Aw, look at you two," Deuce said, stopping beside his own locker. "Together again. You two are harder to separate than my eyebrows! So, Dina," he continued, "what time's our movie date this afternoon?"

Dina started to answer him, but Tinka interrupted her. "I had plans this afternoon," she explained loftily. "We're going tonight. Seven o'clock. I snagged us tickets for the three-D showing."

Dina smiled at her new gal pal. "They're more expensive, but we're worth it, right, Tinky?"

The two girls laughed together.

Deuce was less amused. "Wait, wait a minute," he managed. "Tinky's coming with us?" Both girls smiled and nodded. "Honey," Deuce asked

Dina, "can I talk to you for a second?" He gestured off to the side, and with a shrug Dina got up and joined him. Behind her, Tinka returned to the catalog.

"What's the deal?" Deuce asked once Dina was next to him. He kept his voice down so Tinka wouldn't hear. "For the past two days she's been like a third wheel. Eating with us, studying with us. What happens after the movie when I try to kiss you good night? Are you *both* gonna slap me in the face?" He wasn't looking forward to that!

Dina wasn't all that concerned. "But, sweetie," she explained happily, "I really like having a new girlfriend. And it was all your idea."

Deuce forced himself to let go of his irritation. "Ah, you're right." Besides, if Dina was happy, then he was happy. "I'm sorry," he told her. "You wanna kiss and make up?" He leaned in and puckered up hopefully.

Instead, Dina playfully slapped his cheek. "Deucie," she said, giggling, as she turned away. "Not in school!"

♪ ♪ ♪

Meanwhile, Flynn stood in his living room. He checked to make sure all the pieces were in place. CeCe's old Quickie Bake Oven? Check. The piping hot chocolate-chip cookie he'd just baked in it? Check. Handheld fan? Check. He took the cookie, held it in front of the fan, and aimed the fan toward the open apartment door. It was showtime!

The fan whirred in his hand, sending the smell of fresh-baked cookie out into the hall. Flynn waved his arms to help it along. "Come on, Quickie Bake Oven!" he said softly. "Work your magic!"

Then he set the cookie back in the oven's tray, hid the fan, and rushed over to the couch, where he picked up the TV remote and pretended he'd just been relaxing there the whole time.

Out in the hall, he heard the click of another apartment door opening. Perfect! Sure enough, a second later he saw Freckles stick his head out. Like a curious cat, Freckles sniffed the air. He glanced about, saw the cookie sitting there invitingly on its tray, and smiled.

And then he stepped into the apartment.

"Oh, hey, Freckles," Flynn called out, doing his best to look surprised to see his new neighbor there. "I didn't realize I left the door open. Just testing my sister's old Quickie Bake Oven. Takes six hours to make one cookie, but I don't mind the *commitment*." Then he smiled. "Want one?"

"My mind says no," Freckles started, unable to take his gaze off the cookie, "but who cares what my mind says? I'm hungry!" He picked it up and took a little nibble.

"So, while you're enjoying your organic fruit juice–sweetened cookie," Flynn commented, "perhaps you'd like to check out one of my thousand channels." He waved the remote like it was a magic wand–which, in a way, it was.

Freckles's eyes widened. Without even realizing it, he took a few steps forward. "You get a thousand channels?" he asked, amazed.

"Yeah," Flynn replied, "even though I'm really more of a *one*-channel kind of guy. It even gets foreign stations. You haven't lived till you've seen *The Flintstones* in Italian." He put on his best Italian accent and shouted, "Yabboli dabboli doo!" He was hilarious, and he knew it.

Freckles was clearly torn. "Well," he said slowly, "I guess I could watch for a few *minutos*!" And he rushed over to sit on the couch next to Flynn.

Flynn smiled. "I knew it would work," he muttered to himself.

"Excuse me?" Freckles asked.

Flynn chuckled. "Oh, nothing." He turned on the TV, and soon the two of them were laughing like LTBFFs!

CHAPTER 6

"ALL RIGHT," CECE CALLED out, "five, six, seven, eight!"

She and Rocky, now both wearing Spirit Squad uniforms of their own, watched as the other girls performed their new routine. They actually seemed to be enjoying themselves, and it showed! When they'd finished, all the girls were smiling and clapping, and CeCe clapped with them.

"Yay!" she cheered. Then she nudged her best friend and co-choreographer. "Not bad, huh, Rocky?"

"No, not bad," Rocky agreed. She turned back to the other girls, suddenly scowling fiercely. "Terrible!" That stopped all of them dead in their tracks—including CeCe. But Rocky wasn't finished. "Did any of you practice at all last night?" she demanded.

"I would have," Margie replied, "but you kept us here past my bedtime."

Rehearsal had run pretty late, CeCe thought. But Rocky was determined that the girls get this right.

Crystal spoke up. CeCe and Rocky had already discovered that she and Margie were the leaders of the pack—or had been, before they arrived. "This routine is too hard," Crystal complained. "Why are there so many steps?"

"Eight," Rocky corrected sharply. "It's eight

steps! When CeCe and I were on *Shake It Up, Chicago*, we had to learn a whole new dance every week."

"Again with the *Shake It Up, Chicago*?" Margie muttered loud enough for everyone to hear.

"I wish she would 'shut it up, Chicago,'" Crystal replied with a big smile. She hadn't bothered to lower her voice at all.

"Maybe we should just take a five-minute break," CeCe suggested. She wanted to support her best friend, but she could see that the other girls were one spin away from all-out rebellion.

But Rocky wasn't having it. "No!" she insisted. "The pep rally is coming up in three days and we have to practice until it's perfect!" She glared at the rest of the squad. "Or at least until it's good enough."

Immediately the other girls went into their old routine. "Good enough!" they chanted with the same lack of spirit they'd always shown before. Though slightly better rhythm. "Good enough! Good e–"

Rocky looked ready to strangle them. "Would you please stop that!" she shouted.

The girls silenced themselves at once. They actually looked really hurt, too.

CeCe felt bad for them. "Rocky, give them some credit," she urged. "I mean, they're getting better. Margie only fell down twice, and nobody sprained anything this time." That was a big step up, as far as this squad was concerned!

Her friend remained unconvinced. "CeCe," she argued, "this is my big opportunity to dance again, and I'm not going to let them hold me back."

CeCe was amazed to hear the usually sane and selfless Rocky talking this way. Was this the same girl who'd said, just a few days ago, that she really wanted to help the squad members?

"Do you hear yourself?" CeCe asked. "It's all 'me, me, me.' You sound like . . . me!" She had to stop then for a moment, trying to figure out if she had just insulted her friend, herself, or both of them at once.

Whichever it was, it didn't slow Rocky for a second. "All right, back to work, ladies!" she called instead, spinning around to confront the rest of the squad again. "Now this last part, you guys do your spin. Then I step forward, do my big move, and end with the showstopper." She did a little flourish, clearly already picturing it in her head.

Margie tapped her on the shoulder, bringing her back to reality. "And, uh, what do we do?" she asked. "Just stand in the back, picking our tights out of our butts?"

Rocky gave her a shockingly insincere smile as she replied, "That would kind of be a step up from what you're doing now." Behind her,

CeCe was stunned. Who was this harsh, vicious girl? It looked like her best friend, but she sure didn't act like her!

"All right, ladies," Rocky was telling the squad, "get some water, call your families—it's gonna be a long night!"

She stomped off toward the locker rooms.

As soon as Rocky was out of the gym, Crystal and Margie approached CeCe.

"CeCe," Crystal told her with a big smile, "the girls and I have unanimously voted you as president of the squad!"

"Oh, yay!" CeCe cheered. She hadn't expected anything like this! She smiled wide and tossed her hair back. "So what exactly does the squad president have to do?" She was hoping it involved being in a parade. She loved parades!

"Well, for starters," Crystal answered, her own smile vanishing as if by magic, "fire her."

CeCe stared at her. "Really?" The two other

girls nodded, and she sighed. "Okay, that's easy. Sorry, Margie, you're out."

Margie looked shocked. So did Crystal.

"No, not Margie," Crystal corrected, putting an arm around her friend. "Rocky."

"Ohhhhh." CeCe felt her stomach drop the way it did right before a big test or a major dance performance. "That's going to be a little bit harder."

♪ ♪ ♪

By the time Rocky returned a few minutes later, CeCe was sitting on the lowest step of the bleachers. Alone.

"All right," Rocky announced as she walked in, water bottle in hand, "I'm fully hydrated and ready to rehearse. Let's go, people!" Glancing around, she realized that it was just her and CeCe. "Where is everyone?"

CeCe glanced down at her hands. "They all went home," she admitted.

Rocky frowned. "Those slackers are lucky that I don't kick them off the squad!"

CeCe tried to laugh, but it didn't come out quite right. "Funny you should say that—" she started, but Rocky cut her off. Another thing that her best friend would normally never do!

"I mean, we're the real dancers," Rocky said proudly. "We could just replace them with streamers and an oscillating fan." She nodded at CeCe, obviously expecting her to agree.

But CeCe wasn't going to agree with her this time. "Yeah, about that," CeCe started, rising to her feet. "Everyone who's still on the squad, please do a double pirouette forward." She put a hand on Rocky's shoulder as her friend shifted into motion. "Not so fast, Rocky."

Rocky wasn't in the mood for games. "CeCe, what's going on?" she demanded.

CeCe couldn't bring herself to say it directly. Instead she said, "Well, you know how everyone says that there's no 'I' in team? It turns out, there's no 'u' either." Her voice trailed off. She couldn't look her best friend in the face.

Fortunately, Rocky got the picture. "I'm kicked out?" she asked incredulously. "I'm kicked out?"

CeCe let out a sigh of relief. "Oh, thank goodness you finally got it," she said. "I was running out of cute ways to tell you!"

"But why?" Rocky asked. She honestly didn't understand.

CeCe felt she owed her best friend the truth. "Well, remember how you gave them that motivational speech about how everyone on the squad deserves a shining moment?" she answered. "Yeah, you kind of stole that shining moment for yourself."

For a second, neither of them said anything. Then, to break up the silence, CeCe added, "But it's not all bad news. Guess who got elected squad president?"

Rocky glared at her, and CeCe's happy laugh died away. It looked like they hadn't needed to try out for community theater after all—their lives were already full of drama!

CHAPTER 7

"HI, YOU GUYS READY to order?" Deuce asked as he approached one of the tables at Crusty's, his ordering pad in hand. The three at the table started to respond, but stopped when they noticed him staring up at the ceiling. They looked up as well.

"There's nothing up there," Deuce assured them. "I just tweaked my neck sitting in the front row at the movies while my girlfriend and her new best buddy enjoyed the three-D experience from the best seats in the house." He laughed as best he could. "But am I bitter?" he asked. His laughter turned into a growl. "Darn right I am."

Just then Tinka entered the pizza parlor. In typical Tinka fashion she was wearing leopard print again, this time as a short dress over hot-pink tights and under a short teal jacket.

"I am Tinka!" she announced flamboyantly.

"And I am Dina," Dina added, stepping up right behind her wearing the exact same outfit!

"And we are," the two girls declared together, "sisters from different misters!" They held out their arms as if expecting applause.

Deuce couldn't take it any longer. "Don't throw up, it'll get in your eyes," he warned himself. "Don't throw up, it'll get in your eyes." Then he called out, "Dina, can we talk? Alone?"

Dina turned to Tinka, who looked disappointed. But Dina held up a hand pleadingly, and Tinka finally nodded and crossed toward an empty booth.

Deuce led Dina over to an empty table on the other side. "What's wrong?" she asked him.

"Well, at first . . ." he started, still unable to even see her. His neck was killing him!

Dina realized what was going on, because she stopped him. "Just one second." Then she climbed up on a chair. Now they were face to face.

"At first," he tried again, "I was afraid Tinka was becoming our third wheel, but now I just realized *I'm* the third wheel!"

"Well, you know," Dina told him, still smiling, "the third wheel is the most important wheel on a tricycle!" Obviously she didn't get how much this was upsetting him.

Deuce decided to lay it all on the line. "I can't take this anymore," he said honestly. "I miss my girlfriend. It's either Tinka or me."

"You're making me choose?" Dina asked with surprise.

Part of him wondered if this was a bad idea, but Deuce figured he was committed now. "I'm making you choose," he confirmed.

"Fine!" Dina told him. "I choose Tinka!"

She snorted, hopped down off the chair, and stormed off after her new best friend.

Deuce was left standing there, staring up into the empty space where his girlfriend had been just seconds before. When he'd still had a girlfriend. "Wow," he admitted out loud, "that did not go the way I thought it would."

CHAPTER 8

BACK AT FLYNN'S apartment, Flynn and Freckles were playing video games in Flynn's living room for what felt like ages. Flynn was bored out of his skull, but his new best friend didn't seem in any hurry to leave.

Finally, Flynn commented as casually as he could, "Wow, we've been playing for hours, and it's getting pretty late."

That at least made Freckles pause and lower

the video game controller. "You're right," he said. Then he grinned. "I'll ask my mom if I can sleep over."

Sleep over? Oh, no! But Flynn played it cool. "I don't know," was all he said. "If I don't get a full sixteen hours of shut-eye, I am a wreck in the morning!"

Somehow Freckles saw through him, though. "There it is," he declared. "I knew it was coming. The revolving door is spinning again."

"No, I was just thinking of you!" Flynn protested. He gave Freckles a friendly shove on the arm. "Who wants a grumpy LTBFF?"

That seemed to reassure his friend, for now. "Oh, good." He was all smiles again. "Speaking of which, it's only another three weeks till our one-month friend-iversary!"

Flynn tried to avoid sighing. "Has it only been a week?" he muttered. "Feels longer."

Freckles apparently took that as a good thing.

"I know!" he agreed. "Oooh, and we should really decide which sleepaway camp we're going to this summer. We wanna make sure we're in the same bunk."

Flynn had heard enough. "Whoa, slow down! Sleepaway camp?" This kid was going overboard!

"What's the problem?" Freckles demanded. "Too big a commitment for you?"

Yes, Flynn wanted to scream. *Yes, it is!* But there was no way he was going to admit defeat after all he had been through. "No," he insisted instead. "I am totally one-hundred-percent committed to this friendship!"

"So we're definitely on for tomorrow?" Freckles asked slowly.

Flynn smiled as big as he could. "Pinochle marathon with your grandparents. Can't wait!"

Freckles jumped up from the couch and headed for the front door. Relieved, Flynn followed him. He'd thought this day would never end!

"Pinochle, pinochle, pinochle!" Freckles chanted as he marched to the door. "Aren't you excited?"

"I'll be counting the minutes!" Flynn assured him. "See you tomorrow!"

"See ya!" Freckles agreed.

Then the door was closed and Flynn could finally relax. Man, being an LTBFF was harder than he'd thought!

Then the phone rang. "Hello?" Flynn answered. When he heard who it was, he perked right up. "Oh, hey, Jermaine. What's up?" This time his smile was genuine. "Parasailing? With you and your dad?" Flynn exclaimed. Now they were talking *real* fun! "When do we set sail?" His spirits sank with the answer, however. "Tomorrow?" He paused. "Can you hold on?"

Holding the phone to his chest so Jermaine wouldn't hear, Flynn started weeping like a little baby.

After a second, he put the phone to his face again. "Just one more second," he insisted in a normal voice.

Then he lowered it and started sobbing again.

CHAPTER 9

THE NEXT DAY ROCKY was all alone at her locker. CeCe was off with her new pals—the rest of the Spirit Squad—getting ready for the big rally. Trying not to think about it, Rocky took a book from her locker, crossed to one of the nearby couches, and sat down. She'd just read a bit to take her mind off everything.

But the couch had a half wall behind it, and Deuce happened to pass by on the other side.

"Hey," he called when he spotted Rocky there. He stopped and leaned on the wall. "You going to the pep rally?"

"Why should I?" Rocky snapped, closing the book to look up at her friend. "To be with people who don't want me around?"

"Hey, that's my problem too!" Deuce told her.

"I tried to help the Spirit Squad," Rocky explained to him, letting her anger and frustration finally bubble to the surface. "And they repay me by kicking me out!"

Deuce nodded. "Dina and Tinka kicked me out, too!" he said.

"Why should I go to the pep rally and show my support?" Rocky continued.

"You shouldn't," Deuce told her. "You're doing the right thing. Forget them." At least that's what he was trying to do with Dina.

Rocky considered what he'd said. "So, you agree with me?" she asked slowly.

"One hundred percent," Deuce assured her.

Immediately she rose to her feet and turned to walk away.

"Hey, where are you going?" he asked her.

"To apologize to the Spirit Squad," Rocky explained over her shoulder. "If you think I'm right, I *must* be wrong."

She walked off, leaving Deuce to think about that—and to wonder why it felt like she was right.

♪ ♪ ♪

A few minutes later, Deuce found Dina at the school gym, where everyone was gathering for the pep rally.

"Look, Dina, I'm sorry," he told her before she could blow him off. "I thought I was right and you were wrong, but when I told Rocky *she* was right, I found out *I* was wrong." He thought that made sense. At least, it had in his head!

Dina nodded. "Okay," she replied, "I heard the

word 'sorry' in there, so I'm going to assume that was an apology"—she smiled—"and say all is forgiven, baby."

Deuce relaxed and smiled back. "Great!" He spotted a flash of color near the front of the bleachers. "Look, there's Tinka," he said. "Why don't you go watch the pep rally with her? I'll be fine." He'd rather have Dina some of the time than not at all!

That got an even bigger smile from Dina. "Oh, okay. See you later." She turned to the crowd of students sitting between her and her gal pal. "Make a hole, people!" she announced in typical Dina style. "Make it wide!"

Tinka was sitting and talking with a cute boy when Dina finally reached her. "Hey, Tinka!" Dina called. She turned to the boy. "Move over so I can cop a squat." He did, looking a bit surprised, and Dina sat between them.

Tinka's smile seemed a little strained. "Well, I

was in the midst of canoodling," she commented, "but I guess three's company . . ."

Listening to her, though, Dina realized something. "No, wait," she said. "Three's not company, three's a crowd." She sighed. "Which is what Deuce was saying all along. Gotta go!" She rose to her feet and turned back toward the top of the bleachers. "Make another hole!" she shouted. "Make it wider!"

Tinka returned her attention to the boy. "Thank goodness she got the hint," she whispered. "Now, where were we? Ah, yes." She playfully smacked him across the cheek and giggled. "Not in school!"

Dina, meanwhile, had made her way back over to Deuce. "You know, honey," she told him, "I was thinking. I'd much rather sit with you than Tinka."

"She blew you off, huh?" Deuce asked matter-of-factly.

Instead of being offended, Dina laughed.

"No," she replied, "but this sister missed her mister."

Deuce smiled and put his arm around her. Together, they watched the school mascot dance around on the gym floor. They were almost looking forward to this pep rally!

CHAPTER 10

"OH MY GOSH," Margie declared, peering around the door frame into the gym, "that crowd is huge. It's like the whole school showed up!" Crystal and several of the others peeked alongside her. They were all dressed in sparkly blue-and-orange dresses now, with shimmering silver fingerless gloves and glittery high-tops.

CeCe glanced in from the other side of the doorframe. "That's because it's a pep rally," she explained, unfazed by the number of people she saw there. "And the whole school showed up," she added as the scanned the crowd. "Except for Rocky. I hope she's not too upset. Has anybody seen her?"

Margie shook her head. "No, all I'm seeing is my whole embarrassing life flash before my eyes." She raised one arm. "Like the time I pitted out in front of everybody."

"That's right now, Margie," Crystal warned her. Sure enough, Margie had sweated through the pale blue shirt she had underneath the sleeveless dress.

"We can't do this," she told the other girls. "We're just not ready. We should get out of here." They all nodded, every one of them as panicked as she was.

All except their squad president. "But you guys," CeCe told them, "we're on in five."

"She's right," Crystal said, a smile on her face

as usual. "Hurry, everyone." The smile froze. "Run!"

They all turned to run for it—but just then Rocky stepped into the hall. And she was right in their way!

"Hey, guys," she told them softly. "I just came to say that you were right to kick me off the squad. And I'm really sorry."

CeCe smiled. She could see that her best friend was back to normal.

"Thank you! That means so much," Crystal said. "Now out of the way! We're bailing!"

But Rocky didn't budge. "What?" she asked. "You guys can't give up now. You've worked too hard. Okay, I know you're great, and it's time for everyone out there to know it, too."

"Wow, that's a great speech, Rocky!" CeCe told her. "You put the *spirit* in Spirit Squad!" She saw her chance. "And as your president, I demand that Rocky dance with us!"

Rocky smiled. "Thanks, CeCe. But I don't want to come back unless everyone wants me to." After a pause she added, "Just to be clear, if everyone wants me to, I'm totally willing."

Which was why, a few minutes later, the school band started up, the lights in the gym went out except for a few spotlights, and the entire Spirit Squad sashayed out onto the floor. Including Rocky!

The girls started to dance to the music. They'd replaced the old motto, "Good enough," with a new one: "Anything you can do, I can do better." And as the music played, fun and fast-paced, the girls really got into it! And so did the crowd!

Everyone was clapping along and screaming and whistling when Rocky turned to Margie, who was now next to her in the front row. "Okay, Margie," Rocky told her while still dancing along, "it's time for the showstopper!"

Margie nodded. "Do you want us swaying in

the back," she asked breathlessly, "or can we just go home now?"

But Rocky smiled. "You're not going anywhere," she replied, "because you're doing it!" She took a step to the side so that Margie was now between her and CeCe and dead center to the crowd. "You can't have a shining moment unless you're willing to shine," Rocky told her.

CeCe smiled at her friend over Margie's head. That was the Rocky she knew and loved!

But Margie didn't look convinced. Which was why, CeCe reminded herself, she and Rocky were such a great team.

"Rocky," she explained with a smile, "sometimes life requires more than encouraging words. Sometimes it requires an encouraging *shove!*"

CeCe shoved Margie out in front of all the dancers. For a second, Margie stood there, frozen, with all eyes upon her. Then she started to dance and totally owned her shining moment!

She was great! The rest of the squad mirrored her, but this was definitely Margie's moment, and she ended it with a triumphant split, arms held high! The crowd went wild!

"All right, Margie," Rocky told her after a minute of applause. "You can stop shining now."

The other girl didn't move. "Um, actually, no," she argued, "I can't!"

She was stuck! CeCe and Rocky quickly grabbed her arms and helped her up. Then the whole squad helped her back out. The crowd continued cheering them on the whole way.

♪ ♪ ♪

Back at the apartment, Flynn leaned against the open doorway, arms crossed, waiting. Finally, he saw a familiar dark-haired, bespectacled figure coming down the hall.

"Oh, hey, Flynn," Freckles said as he approached. But Flynn wasn't having any of that. "Don't

'Hey, Flynn' me!" he shouted. "I spent all afternoon playing pinochle with your grandparents, and you never showed. You didn't call, you didn't text!" So much for commitment, he thought.

His so-called LTBFF just smiled. "Gee, Flynn. Don't be so clingy. Something came up. Jermaine from school invited me to go parasailing!"

Flynn stared at him. "Jermaine?" he repeated. "Invited you?"

Freckles nodded. "Apparently there was a last-minute opening." He shrugged. "I didn't think you'd mind, since only a loser would choose pinochle over that!"

Flynn nodded. It was important to keep his cool here. His reputation depended upon it. "Can you hold on one second?" he asked. Then he backed through his apartment door, shut it behind him—and began crying like a baby.

Finally, he collected himself enough to step back out into the hall, where Freckles stood, waiting. "Just one more second," Flynn told him.

Then he hid behind the door and began weeping some more.

He'd never trust an LTBFF again!